LAD, A DOG

Lad to the Rescue

Retold by Margo Lundell

Based on the book by Albert Payson Terhune

Illustrated by Don Bolognese

Hello Reader! — Level 4

SCHOLASTIC INC. Cartwheel B·O·O·K·S ®

New York   Toronto   London   Auckland   Sydney

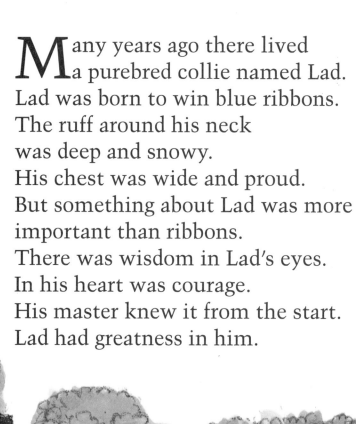

Many years ago there lived
a purebred collie named Lad.
Lad was born to win blue ribbons.
The ruff around his neck
was deep and snowy.
His chest was wide and proud.
But something about Lad was more
important than ribbons.
There was wisdom in Lad's eyes.
In his heart was courage.
His master knew it from the start.
Lad had greatness in him.

Lad lived with his master and mistress
in a big house in the country.
Lad loved the mistress dearly.
But he lived to obey the master.
The master's word was the law.

SPLASH!
Life at the Place was wonderful.
On hot summer days Lad jumped in
the lake and rolled in the cool marsh.
There were acres and acres of woods.
Lad ran free and happy.

One spring, houseguests arrived.
Lad did not like guests.
They always wanted to pat
the big collie and shake his paw.

The law said Lad had to be polite
to all guests on the Place.
But he tried to stay out of their way.
Lad stood back that spring morning
as he watched the guests arrive.
The woman seemed nervous.
The child in her arms looked sickly.

The truth was that the child had been very ill.
When the illness finally went away, the little girl could no longer walk.
The poor thing was thin and pale.
Lad's heart went out to her.
When the child saw Lad that first day, her weak arms reached for him.
"Keep the dog away!" the mother cried. "He will hurt her."
"Never," said the mistress calmly. "Lad would not harm a hair on her head."

In fact, Lad adored the child.
After the first day, no one could keep
the two of them apart.
They spent hours and hours together.

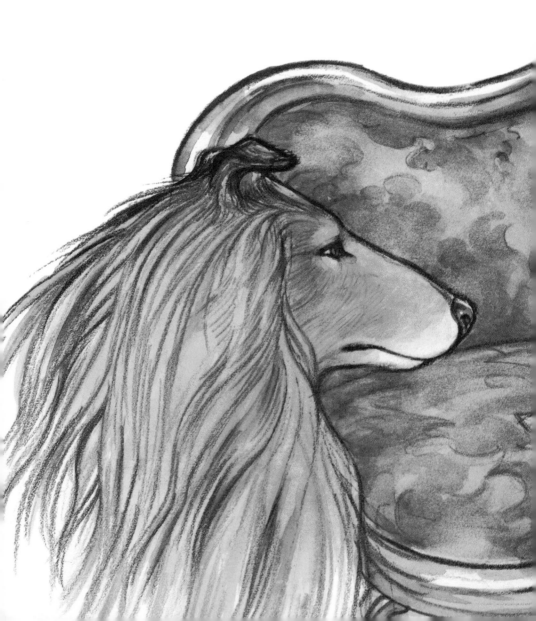

"Doggie, I love you,"
the child would say.
Lad let her pull his big head close
for a kiss.

Lad let the child make him look
silly, too.
He let her dress him up.
He acted in the plays
she put on.
Lad stayed with the child
while she ate her meals.
He even slept outside her door
at night.

The weeks passed.
Little by little the child grew stronger.
Then came a hot day in June.
The mother took the child outside
to wheel her down to the pond
below the house.

Lad went along,
but he was not happy.
He knew that there was danger
down the hill.
He tried to stop the child's wheelchair.
"Out of the way, Lad!" the mother said.

There was a breeze by the pond.
"We shall be cooler here,"
the child's mother said.
She settled her daughter on the grass.
Behind the girl was a low stone wall.

Lad was worried.
He knew that snakes lived in the wall.
He wished the master would come.
The master would warn the guests
about the snakes.
But the master was not home.

At last they heard the car
coming up the long driveway.
The master and mistress were
returning from the post office.
Lad's eyes grew brighter.
His tail thudded against the blanket.
"The mail is here!" the child's mother
said. "I will go see if there is anything
for us. I'll be right back."

The mother stood up quickly,
brushing against the stone wall.
Then she hurried up the hill.

When the mother brushed
against the wall, loose stones rattled
down inside.
The stones fell on a copperhead snake
that was sleeping.
The snake woke up and slowly oozed
out of the wall into the sunlight.

Lad saw the snake and stood up.
Collies are not easily frightened.
But all collies are afraid
of poisonous snakes.
Lad saw the copperhead and felt sick
with fear.
He wanted to run away.

The copperhead flicked its tongue.
It crawled closer to the child.
"Bad snake!" the frightened girl cried.

But she could not run away.
She could not move her legs.
Suddenly, she threw a picture book
at the snake.
The book missed the reptile.
But the copperhead thought
it was being attacked.
In a flash the snake pulled
its head back to strike the girl.

The child called for help.
"Mama! Mama!"
Lad would not let the snake hurt the child.
He threw his mighty body across hers and met the reptile head on.

The copperhead struck.
Its fangs sank deep into Lad's muzzle
and delivered their poison.
The pain was terrible,
but Lad made no sound.

Quickly Lad turned to the child.
He grabbed her gently by the shoulder
with his jaws.
He dragged her farther
from the snake.
Then he whirled around
to face the enemy again.
Lad charged at the coiled snake.
The copperhead was ready
and struck once more.
This time its fangs found Lad's jaw.
The wounded collie did not stop.
He wrestled and fought with the snake
until it was dead at last.

The battle was over.
Lad had been bitten twice.
Soon the brave dog would feel
the deadly poison.
He went and stood over
the crying child.
He began to lick her face.

"No! No! Stop!"
The child's mother raced down
the hill, screaming at the collie.
She had heard the child's cries.
She had seen Lad knock the child over
and drag her across the grass.
The frightened mother was sure
Lad was attacking her little girl.

Suddenly, Lad felt a terrible blow
to his head.
The child's mother had hit him with the
heavy handle of her sunshade.
The frantic mother was protecting
her child.
"No, Mama, don't!" the child begged.
"Mama, he kept the snake away!"
The child cried and pleaded,
but the mother hit Lad again.

The child had to stop the beating.
She had to save Lad.
Somehow she pulled herself to her feet
and took a few awkward steps.
"Mama, stop! Oh, please!" she cried,
grabbing her mother's skirt.
The mother stared at her sobbing child
and let the sunshade fall to the ground.
Her child had *walked.*
The woman could not believe her eyes.
The master arrived just in time to see
the miracle happen.

The mother wept.
She had thought her daughter
would never walk again.
But the child's illness had not injured
her spine.
It had only sapped her strength.
A shock brought back some
of the power the girl had lost.

The master felt joyful for the child.
"Tell us what happened," he urged.
"And what about Lad?"
The child pointed to the dead snake.
She told how Lad had saved her.
The mother felt a terrible sadness.
She had beaten the dog
who had saved her child's life.

After Lad fought the snake, he went
away and hid.
The master looked for him for hours.
"Laddie, come. Here, Lad," he called.
The master felt an urge to cry.
He knew that Lad had probably been
bitten by the snake.
Maybe more than once.
He knew the collie might be very sick
from the poison.
If Lad were dying, the collie would crawl
deep into the woods by himself.

For the next several days the child was
busy learning to walk again.
But she missed Lad all the time.
"Where is he?" she wailed.

On the fourth day the master started
out for a walk by himself.
It was early in the morning.
The master's heart was heavy.
Lad had always kept him company
on his morning walks.

On the porch
a strange, lumpy figure
lay curled on the rug.
In the dim light it was hard to see.

As the master came out on the porch,
the figure stirred.
The master walked closer.
"It can't be," he whispered.
Then the caked and filthy animal
lifted his poor head.

Suddenly the master sat on the floor
close to the grimy creature.
He caught him in his arms.
"Lad! Laddie! Old friend!" he sputtered,
half-crying. "You're alive! You're alive."

Lad's body was thin.
His head was swollen.
But the worst of the swelling seemed
to be over.
And from spine to toe, from nose to
tail, Lad was a mass of dried mud.

Later on, everyone wanted to know
how Lad had survived.
The master said Lad probably knew he
would die from the snakebite.
But an ancient part of Lad's brain told
him there was a way to help himself.
He could go into the marsh and bury
himself in mud.
The mud would pull the poison
from his body.

And the long, slow mud bath worked.
"He came out of the marsh a little thin
and shaky," said the master. "But he
came out alive. That's what matters.
Our Lad is very much alive."

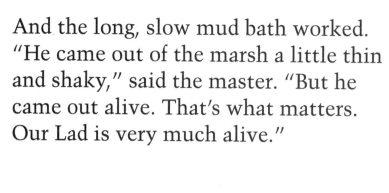

— *About Lad* —

*The famous collie lived with the
talented animal and nature writer,
Albert Payson Terhune, and his wife,
in Pompton Lakes, New Jersey. The
"Place" was a wooded estate called
Sunnybank.*

*A series of magazine stories about Lad
were published during World War I.
The stories were very popular. After the
war, the stories were published in a book.
The book about Lad sold very well.
The brave, loyal dog became so popular
that people would drive to Sunnybank
uninvited "to see where Lad lived."
The author was finally forced to put up
gates and keep them closed.*

*Terhune went on to write stories about
other dogs, but he was always best
known for the tales he told about the
collie. There was no other dog like Lad.
The author said it well in his dedication
to the book:*

This book is dedicated

to the memory of

LAD

thoroughbred in body and soul